The Goffins
Fun and Games

The Goffins
Fun and Games

JEANNE WILLIS
illustrated by Nick Maland

WALKER
BOOKS

To my dear friend Annie and Annie's Mum xx
J.W.

For Sarah, Rune and Rafe, with love
N.M.

First published 2009 by Walker Books Ltd
87 Vauxhall Walk, London SE11 5HJ

2 4 6 8 10 9 7 5 3 1

Text © 2009 Jeanne Willis
Illustrations © 2009 Nick Maland

The right of Jeanne Willis and Nick Maland to be identified as
author and illustrator respectively of this work has been asserted by them
in accordance with the Copyright, Designs and Patents Act 1988

This book has been typeset in ITC Veljovic

Printed and bound in Great Britain by Clays Ltd, St Ives plc

British Library Cataloguing in Publication Data:
a catalogue record for this book is available from the British Library

ISBN 978-1-4063-0870-9

www.walker.co.uk

CONTENTS

THE CARRUTHERS

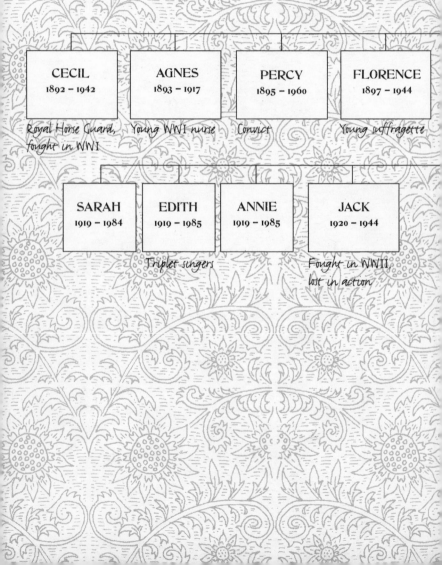

CECIL
1892 – 1942

Royal Horse Guard,
fought in WWI

AGNES
1893 – 1917

Young WWI nurse

PERCY
1895 – 1960

Convict

FLORENCE
1897 – 1944

Young suffragette

SARAH
1919 – 1984

EDITH
1919 – 1985

ANNIE
1919 – 1985

Triplet singers

JACK
1920 – 1944

Fought in WWII,
lost in action

FAMILY TREE

MONTAGUE CARRUTHERS
1870 – 1960
m
MAUD GOODWIN
1871 – 1971

Explorer, sailor, whaling ship

Suffragette, Titanic, WWI Nurse, maid servant called Violet, lived to be 100

SID
1899 – 1975
m
DOLLY GRAY
1900 – 1975

Joined army to fight WWI, under age, lost leg, won medals

VICTORIA
1901 – 1904

GORDON
1922 – 2005
m
PEGGY ELLIS
1926 –

Fought against Hitler in WWII as a young man

MARY
1926 – 2006

Evacuee

FRANK
1928 – 2003

Evacuee

SIMON
1958 –

PHILLIP
1960 –
m
SUSAN DERBYSHIRE
1966 –

Saved child from drowning

GEORGE
1999 –

Discovered Goffins living in his grandma's attic

CHAPTER ONE

BOOTS AND BARKING

Ever since George discovered Lofty and Eave living secretly in his grandmother's attic, the summer holidays had flown by. At first, he wasn't quite sure if they were human. They looked like people, but they weren't like anybody he'd ever met.

Lofty was very short for a man and extremely hairy, and even though Eave insisted she was nine, she was no bigger than a five-year-old. They spoke English, but the way they talked was unlike anything George had heard before. There was a good reason for this: Lofty and Eave were Goffins.

Fun and Games

Their great-great-grandfolk had come from
a tiny island called Inish Goff, which had sunk
into the Irish Sea. These Goffins had escaped
on rafts and, with nowhere else to live, they
had set up home in the roofs of abandoned
buildings. Whole generations of Goffins had
been raised up in the clouds, away from the
prying eyes of Them Below, and only daring
to venture out under the cover of darkness.

According to Lofty, there were Goffins
living in the belfries of crumbling
churches and forgotten follies
all across the country.

There were Goffins in the tops of empty tower blocks, windowless warehouses and the attics of thousands of derelict houses. In fact, George now knew that he was never more than five roofs away from a Goffin.

The Goffins lived in constant fear of being discovered, but so far nobody had found them – or if they had, they'd kept it to themselves, as George had. He'd promised never to tell a soul about Lofty and Eave. Otherwise they'd have to move to a new house and he didn't want to lose the only friends he had right now.

Like all Goffins, Lofty and Eave relied on other people's junk for their survival. They wore a strange mixture of old clothes they'd found in the attic, and had made a cosy home there using odd bits of furniture to create separate rooms: a sitting area, two bedrooms, a bathroom and a kitchen.

All around the walls, Eave
had stuck faded photos of people who
all looked vaguely familiar to George.
When he first saw them gazing back at
him he had no idea who they all were.
They had freaked him out. But then Eave
explained they were his own relatives, going
right back to his great-great-grandparents,
and he was fascinated.

Fun and Games

George had never thought about his ancestors before, but Eave had made them come alive for him. She'd gathered so much information about them from the stashed-away letters, diaries and papers, she'd been able to draw up George's family tree. Now he could see at a glance who they all were, when they were born and who they had married.

Eave had also shown George a battered, leather-bound almanac in which his great-great-grandpa, Montague Carruthers, had recorded all the adventures he'd had when he was an explorer. George spent many happy hours flicking through it with Eave in the little garden she'd made out on the roof.

They could get to the garden by climbing out of the skylight. Eave grew fruit and vegetables there.

When they were
out of season, Lofty
took pot luck and
cast his fishing rod
Down Below and
hooked up half-eaten
cakes, toast crusts
and other scraps that
Grandma Peggy left
out for the birds.

15

Fun and Games

It amazed George how Lofty and Eave managed to live on so little. True, they kept bees, so they had honey, and there was a tame pigeon called Chimbley who laid eggs.

But provisions were always in short supply and as they daren't leave the loft, George did his best to bring them whatever they needed. He had to be careful though. If his mum noticed certain items had gone missing, she'd ask awkward questions. Toilet paper, for example: he couldn't risk taking a whole roll, so he'd pinch half and if she asked why he'd used so many sheets, he'd say he had a stomach upset.

Sometimes he went without dinner to feed Lofty and Eave. He'd eat a few mouthfuls and then, when no one was looking, wrap what was left in a hanky and shove it in his pocket or down his sock – gravy and all – to give to them later.

It was no hardship really. He felt it was doing him good to eat a bit less. When he first arrived at Grandma Peggy's, he'd eaten far too much out of boredom and loneliness. He'd been missing his old friends and he had no brothers or sisters to play with. Even his parents never seemed to have any time for him.

17

Fun and Games

Now George's days were filled. He
was planning to visit Lofty and Eave this
afternoon, but first he had to go shopping
with his mum. She had found a new school for
him to start in September and had promised
to take him into town this morning to buy
him new football boots.

George was really looking forward to it. He
knew exactly which sort he wanted and was
all ready to go when suddenly
the phone rang. His
mother answered it;
when she put the
receiver down
again, she was
looking a bit cross.
"I'm afraid I've
got to go into
work, George."

George's mum was a nurse. The hospital was often short-staffed and she didn't have any choice. George wasn't happy.

"You never put me first," he complained. "Why d'you have to work anyway? Dad's got a job. It's not like we're poor or anything."

His mum sighed. "I'll take you shopping tomorrow, George."

"I don't want to go tomorrow," sulked George. "Can't Dad take me?"

"Dad's busy. He's clearing out the shed."

George pulled a face. Dad was always busy. George had moaned to Lofty about it, but Lofty said it worked both ways; if George took more interest in his dad, maybe his dad would take more interest in him. Well, his dad could take more interest by buying him those boots, couldn't he?

George went down to the bottom of the garden and found his father in the shed. He didn't exactly *look* busy. In fact, he was sitting on a bucket doing a crossword.

"Dad, can you take me shopping
for football boots?"

"Not now, George. This shed's
going to take all morning."

"What about this afternoon then?"

"I can't. I'm going round to Bill's to borrow a ladder and watch the match."

George sucked his teeth and tutted. "And that's more important than taking me to get new boots, is it?"

"It's an important... friendly game," said his dad.

George threw his hands in the air and stormed off. His father called after him. "Instead of sulking, it would be nice if you kept Grandma company."

"Fine!" George yelled back.

It wasn't that George didn't like Grandma. They'd been getting on much better from the moment he suspected she knew about Lofty and Eave. She'd never admit it, but she always managed to cause a diversion if his dad threatened to go anywhere near the attic. George picked up one of his toys and ambled off to visit her. His parents had turned the room facing the garden into a granny bedsit now that she couldn't manage the stairs.

Fun and Games

George had grown very fond of Grandma, even though she was grumpy sometimes; maybe he'd inherited his grumpiness from her. It was soon clear, however, that if George thought *he* was in a bad mood, Grandma was in an even worse one. She was lying on top of the duvet pulling a face. He'd brought his Robodog to show her.

It was a robotic dog that obeyed when he gave
certain commands. It could sit, walk and wag
its tail. It could even dance. But Grandma
wasn't impressed at all.

"Stop that blessed thing barking, boy!"
she snapped.

"Thought you liked dogs, Grandma. That's
why I brought it to show you."

"I like real dogs – not metal ones that need
batteries. What's the point of a dog like that?
You can't stroke it. It doesn't love you."

"You don't have to take it for walks," said
George.

Grandma rolled her eyes. "Walks? Chance would be a fine thing. My knees are killing me, boy."

"Well, is there anything you *do* want to do, Grandma?" asked George, hoping there wouldn't be.

"What about a parlour game?" she asked. "A decent game. Like I used to play when I was a girl."

George wasn't sure what a parlour was, let alone a parlour game, so he shook his head. "I don't think I know any, Grandma."

She looked disappointed. "What, none? Oh, forget it. I might as well go back to sleep."

Grandma stared out at the garden through the French windows, then closed her eyes.

"I was s'posed to get new football boots today," muttered George.

"It always has to be new with you, boy," sighed Grandma. "The old things are the best."

George considered arguing with her but as she was determined to go to sleep, his dad

was in the shed
and his mum
was at work, it
seemed a good
time to visit Lofty
and Eave. Maybe
they'd appreciate
his Robodog.

Chapter Two

SPILLIKINS AND SUFFRAGETTES

George went up to his room and knocked on the small green door opposite his bed, which led to the attic. He used a secret code so that Lofty and Eave knew it was him.

Pom ... tiddy pom pom ... pom pom!

Eave opened the door cautiously. She was wearing a Victorian maid's outfit that swamped her tiny frame, and a lace cap that fell down over her gooseberry-green eyes. She pushed it back and wiped her hands on the frilly apron, which frothed around her ankles. When she saw George, her freckly face split into a huge smile.

"Goodly morn, Jowge!" she said. "Howfor be yourself?"

"What on earth are you dressed like that for, Eave?"

"Us has been cleanin'," she giggled. "Thus myneself be wearin' Missy Violet's pinny ... herself be your great-great-grandmuppy Maud's servant, yay?"

"I remember you telling me," George replied. A hundred years ago, George's bedroom had belonged to Violet, the family servant. Fortunately, he didn't sleep in her bed – that had been stored in the attic a long time ago.

Just then, Eave noticed George's Robodog. "Jowge Carruthers!" she exclaimed. "Whyfor has yourself be-fetched us a metal hound?"

She looked at it
curiously, then poked it
with her feather duster. It began
to bark robotically. As soon as he heard the
unfamiliar noise, Lofty crept out from behind
a totem pole, flapping his arms and shushing.

29

Fun and Games

"Trash and hide,
Littley! Be-snuff
yonder candils afore
Them Below be
cotching us!"

He was trying to
get Eave to help him
scatter the furniture
and ornaments
in a desperate
attempt to make
the attic look
unoccupied.

"Don't panic, Lofty ... it's OK," said George.
"It's not a real dog. It's a toy, see?"

He flicked the off switch and stopped it
barking. "Anyway, Mum's out, Dad's
in the shed and Grandma's fast
asleep. No one can hear us."

Lofty heaved a sigh of
relief and slumped down on
a faded lilac chaise longue

that was in the part of the loft the Goffins had converted into a sitting area. It was furnished with all sorts of fascinating objects including a stuffed crocodile with a large toothy grin.

"Your lounge is much more interesting than ours," said George.

"Lahhhnge?" laughed Eave, mimicking his accent. "Nay, this be us parlour, Jowge!"

"So that's what a parlour is," said George. "The posh room where you sit and entertain your friends?"

31

Fun and Games

"Yay! Come
sit! Myneself will be
learnin' you some games,
yay?" replied Eave. She ushered him
past the portrait of his great-great-grandfather
Montague fighting a polar bear and settled
him down next to Lofty. By his feet was a
pile of old-fashioned board games. George
recognized ludo and Monopoly but none of
the rest.

"Myneself and Pappy be rarin' to play!" said Eave. "Does yourself be knowin' Spillikins, Jowge?"

"Spillikins? Never heard of it," said George.

Lofty reached into the box and pulled out a well-worn cardboard tube, decorated with a picture of a rosy-cheeked family having riotous fun playing Spillikins around a table. He flipped the metal lid

off and tipped the contents onto the table; it was full of miniature weapons. There were axes, lances, arrows, guns, knives and swords

all carefully carved out of bone – or was it ivory? Even Lofty wasn't sure.

Fun and Games

"Darst say your great-great-grandpappy Montague be-scovered this game abroad," he said. "'Tis from the Orient."

George toyed with the pile of miniature weapons on the table. "So ... how do we play?" he asked.

"Us must be choosin' and pickin' up a weapon without disturbin' the others," Eave explained. The game of Spillikins began. It wasn't as easy at it looked and George lost. He wasn't normally a sore loser, but it had been a bad morning so he was quite sulky about it.

"Play again!" insisted Eave. "Yourself be surely winnin' this time, Jowge."

"No," he said. "I can't be bothered."

Eave looked confused. "Whyfor be yourself frownin' Jowge?"

"I'm not frowning!" he snapped.

Eave's lip trembled. She pulled her maid's cap off and started sobbing into the lace. "Alack! Whyfor be myne oh-nee friend angry with myneself?"

George felt awful. What kind of bully was he, making little girls cry? He couldn't bear to see her so upset.

"Hey ... I'm sorry, Eave." He dabbed at her tears with the fluffy drawstring on his sweatshirt. "I'm not angry with you. I'm just in a rubbish mood today, OK?"

Eave blew her nose on her cap and put it back on her head. "Whyfor be yourself full of miseree, Jowge?"

George explained about the football boots and how cross he was with his mum. "She promised to take me shopping but she had to go to work." He said the bit about her going to work quite sarcastically. "Why can't she stay at home and be a housewife like a proper mum?" he groaned.

There was an awful silence. Lofty and Eave were staring at him in horror.

"What?" he sighed. "What have I said now?"

otographs

as Netticoats

Irkwipment

m Relic

Eave got up and
marched over to the
wall by the green door.
Boxes and cases filled
with his relatives'
old belongings were
stacked to the roof. She
had sorted through
and labelled
everything
in her own
handwriting.

"Fie! Yourself has riled myne Eave, Jowge!"
said Lofty.

"Why, Lofty? What have I said to upset her?"
Surely she couldn't be angry with him just for
saying he wished his mum didn't work?

Lofty sucked in his cheeks and narrowed
his eyes. "'Tis a dreadfil sin for a Goffin to
be badmouthin' a muppy, Jowge. A muppy
be labourin' most tireless for her fambily.
Without herself, where would themselves be?"

Eave returned, struggling with a large
leather trunk. George tried to help her,
but she scowled and batted him
away with her hand.

"Nay thanklee!
Myneself be
a-managin' by
myne ownself!"
At which point
she tripped over
her frilly apron and
landed on her bottom.

Fun and Games

George did his utmost not to laugh
and pulled her back up. As soon as she'd
scrambled back onto her feet, she let go of his
hands and wagged her finger at him furiously.

"Jowge, howfor darst yourself be whingin'
about your muppy toilin' and a-labourin'?"

George tried to defend himself. "All I'm
saying is I don't know why she has to go
to work. She's got enough to do, what with
looking after the house and Grandma. That's
why we moved here in the first place."

George had always thought of work as a
bad thing – something you had to do to make
money. But it had never crossed his mind that
his mother might actually enjoy her job.

"And your mum doesn't work, does she,
Eave?" he continued. "You told me she had to
look after your granny in the church belfry!"

Eave shook her head so hard her maid's cap
flew off. "Myne muppy Ariel be doin' both,
Jowge!" she exclaimed. "Herself be carin' for
Granny Cloister with myne oh-nee brother

Arch, but be-nights, herself be healin' sicklee Goffins."

"Really?" said George. "She's a nurse, like my mum?"

Lofty folded his arms and puffed out his chest proudly. "Myne Ariel be a fine doctor, Jowge. Herself be Doctor Ariel Steeple!"

"All Goffin laydees be mostly havin' jobs, Jowge," said Eave. "But not for munnee. Goffins never be usin' munnee, as yourself knows. Us be swappin' goods and skills or us be doin' things for a Kindness. Until ten summers past, Granny Cloister be workin' as a Judge."

"Why don't you use our doctor and judges?" asked George.

Lofty frowned deeply and shook his head. "Yourself be forgettin' that all Goffins be livin' on this isle in secret! Us doesn't exist in the eyes of Them Below. Ourselves has no dockyments to say us has even been borned."

"Or deaded," interrupted Eave. "Them

Down Below is never treatin' peepil without dockyments, Jowge."

"Yay," continued Lofty, "as for usin' your judgin's, nay! Us can oh-nee be judged by a Goffin as ourselves does live by most different rules."

"Us has our own dentipeeps, too. Myneself is plannin' on bein' a dentipeep one fine day," said Eave, gnashing her teeth at him. They were all still her baby ones by the looks of it.

George looked her up and down. She'd tried her best to pin, tuck and hem the maid's uniform she was wearing but none of the clothes she'd found in the attic ever fitted her properly.

"Do you have Goffin dressmakers?" he asked.

She wrinkled up her nose and laughed. "Nay, whyfor be us needin' a dressinmaker? Myneself be masterly at sewin' and a-stitchin'. Myneself be alterin' this normous uniform with a niddle and cottin, Jowge. 'Tis hard to tell, yay?"

"Er ... yay," said George. "You've made it look ... great." He'd already hurt her feelings once today. He didn't want to do it again. He helped her put the heavy trunk on the table and sat down on the chaise longue.

"Myneself be comin' from a fambily of workin' ladydee folk, Jowge," she said. "Themselves be owlwise and oxstrong and most deservin' of respect. Indeed, myne great-great-grandmuppy Steeple be the first laydee Ruler of Inish Goff. In yestertimes, your great-great-grandmuppy Carruthers be a most famous workin' laydee also..."

"You mean Great-Great-Grandma Maud?" interrupted George. "She was the one who married Great-Great-Grandpa Monty, right?"

"Yay, and herself did have six bubbies. Themselves be called Cecil, Agnes, Percy, Florence, Sid and Victoria— "

"And she had a servant called Violet!" finished George. "Cor, it must be great to have a servant. Lazy, lazy Great-Great-Grandma!"

41

Fun and Games

Eave snapped open the catches on the suitcase. "Jowge, don't darst be callin' Great-Great-Grandmuppy Maud layzee! Herself did tigerfight for the right to be a workin' laydee!"

The trunk was full of old newpaper articles. Eave pulled out a copy of *The Times* and smoothed it out on the table. It was dated 15th February 1912. On the front page, there was a photo of several angry-looking women dressed in bonnets and long dresses. They appeared to be chained to some railings outside a public building. Eave pointed to a handsome young woman in the middle. She was the smallest, but she looked very determined.

"That be Maud!" she said. "Herself be lookin' most feisty!" George peered at the face in the photo. It was a bit blurred, but it was definitely his great-

great-grandma. He recognized her features from an oil painting that was resting on an artist's easel.

"Who chained her up?" asked George. "Was it the police? Was she a criminal?"

Eave shook her head so hard, her cap came off again and her wild, red plaits unravelled and sprang out in corkscrews.

"Nay! Maud be chainin' herself up! Herself be a Sufferin' Jet!"

"A suffering what?"

43

Fun and Games

A suffragette. George had learnt a bit about the suffragette movement at school – it was something to do with women fighting for equality, as far as he could remember – he hadn't really been listening. He had done a topic about them but he hadn't paid much attention because he couldn't see how anything that happened in the past could possibly have anything to do with him. But now he could – his family was involved!

He began to read the article. It said that Maud Carruthers, along with several other suffragettes had set fire to post boxes and chained themselves to the railings to protest about women not being allowed to vote or have careers. George was surprised.

"Weren't allowed? Why not?" It seemed daft. His mum had always voted and always worked. He couldn't imagine anyone telling her what to do, least of all his dad.

"Long-a-long times past, iggerant men be-thunk laydeefolk be oh-nee fit for havin' bubbies and bakin' buns," said Lofty. "But 'twas never the Goffin way."

"Goffins be borned eekwill, laydees and genteelmen," added Eave.

George read on and gasped. "Ugh! Oh, that's horrible!" He clutched his throat, gagging. Lofty thought he was choking and smacked him sharply between the shoulder blades.

"Alack! Has yourself gargled a moth, Jowge?"

"Ouch! No ... read that bit, Lofty! It's horrid. Poor Great-Great-Grandma!"

It said that Maud had been arrested and put in Holloway Prison. She'd gone on hunger strike and the wardens had force-fed her through a tube pushed down her throat.

"Herself be most lionbrave," said Eave. "Be thankly, for Maud and the Sufferin' Jets did bring power to the laydeefolks. Now themselves be rightlee votin' and rulin' and workin', yay?"

George was delighted to learn that his great-great-grandma had been such a rebel and helped to bring equality to women, but he still wished his mother didn't go to work.

"I don't see why she has to have a job," he said. "It's not like we need the money."

Eave threw up her hands. "'Tis not all about munnee, Jowge! Sometimes, us be workin' for fun or for betterin' this world. Your muppy be a nurse, yay? Herself be savin' lives, like myne muppy and Agnes."

"Agnes?"

"Agnes be Maud's daughter, Jowge. Herself be nursin' soldiers in Worldly War One." Eave rooted round in the trunk and produced a small silk box. As she opened it, the tiny hinges squeaked. "Herself did win this in 1917."

It was the Military Medal for Bravery. Despite being badly injured herself, Nurse Agnes Carruthers had given her gas mask to a wounded young soldier and carried on helping the injured. Eave handed George a letter that Agnes had written home.

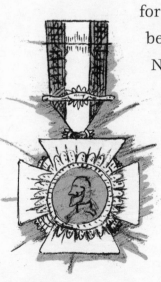

Dear Mother,

I am with the operating team 100 miles from our base hospital, close to the fighting line. I have been here three weeks and see no signs of going back. Of course I didn't bring much with me. Two white dresses, two aprons and two combinations. Can you imagine trying to keep decent when it rains every day? We all live in tents and have to wade ankle-deep through the mud to the operating room. We paint on a cheery smile for the sake of our boys; they are so young and have suffered so much...

"'Twas the lastest letter Agnes be sendin' home to her fambily, Jowge," sighed Eave.

"She made it back, didn't she?"

Eave lowered her head, folded the letter with great care and put it back in the suitcase.

"Alack, herself never did, Jowge. 'Tis most sorrowfill, yay? But thankly to Agnes, many, many soldiers be saved."

George went quiet. He sat there, stroking the medal. Suddenly, saving lives seemed much more important than shopping for football boots. He would never have spoken to his mother like that if he'd known what he knew now.

It was Lofty who broke the silence. "All work and no play doth make a Goffin dull! Thus, myneself be challengin' Jowge to a goodly game of Taw. Or does yourself prefer Cherry Pit?"

CHAPTER THREE

BANDAGES
AND BUTTER

George had never heard of Taw or Cherry
Pit. Lofty thrust his hand into the pockets of
his baggy explorer's shorts and pulled out a
handful of marbles. They were made from
cloudy glass, not a bit like the ones George
had seen in toy shops before. He'd always
wanted a bag of those. They looked so bright
and sparkly but he had no one to play with at
home and marbles had been banned at his old
school after his friend Warren slipped on one
in the boys' toilets and cracked his head on
the loo seat. Lofty shared them out.

"Are these Goffin marbles?" asked George.

Fun and Games

"Nay," said Eave. "Themselves be stoppers from stone bottils of lemmin'-aid which Pappy did find among the loft trove."

"Bottle stoppers?" asked George. "But what do you do with them?"

Lofty pulled back the rug, drew a circle on the bare boards with a lump of chalk and suggested that they play Taw; one of many marble games that he knew.

"To be playin' Cherry Pit, us must be knockin' marbils down holes, but to be playin' Taw, yourself must be knockin' myne marbil beyonder the circle, Jowge."

They dropped down on their hands and knees and began to play. George got quite carried away. He loved the satisfying crack of marble against marble. He was really good at it and when he finally beat Lofty, he found himself leaping up and down on the chaise longue.

"Yourself be a deadilly shot, Jowge!" laughed Eave.

Then George remembered his manners. He'd been a bad loser with Spillikins; maybe he could redeem himself by being an honorable winner and not showing off quite so much. He stopped bouncing, shook Lofty warmly by the hand and tried to sound humble.

"It was just beginner's luck, Lofty."

"Nay, Jowge. Yourself be a champion marbiller, no less!"

53

Fun and Games

George's mood had lifted no end and when Eave suggested that they play a few parlour games he was more than happy to learn; he'd have something to play with Grandma Peggy later.

After a game of I Spy and several rounds of "I'm Thinking of Something" in which Eave thought of an object and everyone had to guess what it was by asking only twenty questions, George decided to teach them Blind Man's Bluff. He'd played it at his fifth birthday party and felt it was his turn to show them something new.

"The idea of this game is to blindfold someone and spin them round. Then they have to try and catch the rest of the players," he explained.

"Won't us be dreadfill dizzy?" asked Eave.

"Yeah. That's the fun part," said George.

Only it wasn't quite as fun as he'd hoped. Having blindfolded Lofty with one of Great-Great-Grandma Maud's old silk scarves, George told Eave to spin her father round and round.

Unfortunately, she spun him too enthusiastically and Lofty began to spin wildly out of control, knocking over the lampshade, bumping into the bookcase and finally falling headfirst into a Grecian urn covered in barnacles.

Fun and Games

"Great-Great-Grandpa Monty did be-scover that normous vase on a shipwreck," said Eave, pointing at Lofty's feet waving in the air. "Himself be divin' for trove and be nearly snuffocated by an ockertypuss."

George grabbed hold of Lofty's ankles. "Never mind that now, help me pull him out!"

By the time they managed to get him upright, his pith helmet was well and truly wedged over his ears. They all took turns to pull it off, but it wouldn't budge.

"Whatever shall us do?" giggled Eave.

"Howfor darst yourself be larfin' at poor Pappy!" wailed Lofty.

"Butter!" cried George. He would go and fetch some butter and grease the helmet off. When he lived in London, his friend Dino had got his head caught between the school railings and the dinner lady had rescued him by rubbing his sticky-out ears with a catering pack of butter from the canteen.

"Hastily, Jowge!" cried Lofty. "Myne ears be most crumpilled! Myne head be throbbin'!"

George ran downstairs to the kitchen and raided the fridge.

Just then, his father came in from the garden and asked him what he was doing with the butter dish.

"Just ... making a sandwich. Want one, Dad?"

57

He wouldn't have offered in the past, but
Eave had taught him that the Goffin way was
to do someone a Kindness whenever you
could, without expecting anything back. But
his dad wasn't hungry.

"No thanks. I'm off to Bill's now. What are
you up to?"

George could hardly tell him he was about
to go up to the attic to grease a Goffin's head
out of a pith helmet, so he said, "Oh ... nothing
much."

"Come with me if you want, then. It'll be
a good game."

George turned him down. He said it was
because his team wasn't playing. He supported
Man United, because all his mates did.

"Another time, Dad, yeah?"

His dad looked quite disappointed. George
felt a pang of guilt; maybe he'd genuinely
wanted his company for once. They always
used to avoid each other on purpose, but since
George had met Eave and seen how close she

was to her dad, he'd been trying to make a bit more effort with his own. Now he'd ruined it by saying he didn't want to watch the football with him – the only time he'd ever been asked.

Oh well. At least he could do the Goffins a Kindness. He fetched an aspirin for Lofty's headache and carried the butter up to the attic. The butter worked a treat. Eave warmed it over a candle and, with Lofty standing on his head to prevent drips, she squirted the frothy yellow oil under the rim of his pith helmet with an old eye-dropper.

It was George's idea to try and twist the helmet off rather than pull, and all the while, Lofty protested as loudly as a Goffin dared.

"Ow! Waaaagh! Yourself be pullin' off myne head, Jowge!"

"Hush, Pappy. Yourself be such a normous bubby!" laughed Eave.

Finally, the helmet came off. Lofty licked the rim, declared that it was besterly butty and George handed him the aspirin.

"Just swallow it with a glass of water," he said. "It'll get rid of your headache."

Lofty looked at the pill suspiciously. He sniffed it then gave it back. "Nay thankly, Jowge. Us be usin' *Goffin* cures for all ills."

"Mostly us be usin' herbs and potions," Eave added. "Willow bark be besterly for curin' head ouch. A hotbottle be soothin' knacky knees, and for hackin' and sneezin', myself be mixin' honnee and lemmin'."

George knew where their honey came from: Lofty collected it from the wild bees who had made their home behind the plaster near the skylight. But how did they get hold of lemons? There was a cherry tree out in the roof garden. Eave had grown it from a stone that her pet squirrel, Roofus, had fetched, but as far as he could remember, there was no lemon tree.

"Myneself does roof-fish for fruitibles such as lemmin's," explained Lofty.

"Grandmuppy Peg be likin' gin
with a splice of lemmin'. Come
summertimes, herself be sittin'
Below, boozin' and snoozin' and
downwards goes myne fishin' hook
and upwards comes the lemmin'!"

"You nick the lemon slices out
of Grandma's gin from right under
her nose? Doesn't she ever notice?"
laughed George.

Lofty shrugged. "That be
dependin' on how many herself
has swiggled, Jowge. And
some a-times herself be
blamin' your pappy
for it."

"Yay!" giggled Eave.
"Us be hearin' Grandmuppy
Peg sayin', 'Phil … lip!
Whyfor be yourself
forgettin' to put lemmin's
in myne gin again?'"

Fun and Games

"You never take Grandma's little brown tablets though, do you?"

"Whyfor be yourself askin', Jowge?"

"They're laxatives ... they give you the ... they make you go to the toilet a lot."

Eave looked at her father who had suddenly gone bright red and was trying to avoid her gaze. "Pappy! No wonder yourself be makin' such a deadily whiff in us closet yester-times! Muppy be-warnin' us never, never to be takin' a non-Goffin cure!"

"'Twas be-accidents," mumbled Lofty. "Myneself be thinkin' 'twas choclick drops."

Eave rolled her eyes and sighed. "Whatfor is myne pappy like, Jowge?"

Lofty muttered apologetically and sidled off.

"Oh, Eave," whispered George. "You've really embarrassed him. His face was scarlet!"

But Eave was unrepentant. "'Tis betterly to be a redded Goffin than a deaded Goffin, Jowge."

George knew she had a point. As a warning, his mother had told him all about the children she'd had to nurse in hospital after they'd made themselves ill by taking tablets they'd mistaken for sweets.

"Our medicine is probably better than yours though," he said. "If you got sick, I could get you some."

"Us won't be needin' it, Jowge," Eave told him. "Goffins be most healthee. Us never be sufferin' from the sickliness like Them Below."

Fun and Games

"But modern medicine has a lot to offer..." said George, rather pompously. It was a phrase he'd heard his mother use.

"Myneself be knowin' that," said Eave patiently. "So some a-time, us must be usin' erkwipment myneself did be-scover in the loft trove." She waved the glass eye-dropper at George to prove her point. "This dripper did belong to Agnes," she said. "'Twas in a Wordly War One nursin' kit."

"Hardly modern then, is it, Eave?"

"Jowge, a dripper be a dripper no matter how many winters old, yay? 'Tis workin' fine!" She padded softly into the gloom then returned a few moments later

carrying a scratched metal
box. It had a red cross
painted on the lid, and
inside there was a
tray packed with all
sorts of medical items
dating from the First
World War. There were rolls of
bandages, surgical tape, steel forceps,
a thermometer in a case and
rusty tins of ointments
and powders.

There was another
tray under the first one.
Along with Agnes' identity
disc and a prayer signed by her
commander-in-chief, there was a needle and
a reel of surgical cotton.
There was a nasty red
stain on it. The sight
of it made George
feel queasy.

Fun and Games

"I hope that was for sewing on buttons," he muttered.

Eave shook her head. "Nay, Jowge. That be for sewin' up soldiers. Myneself darst not be showin' you Agnes' scibblin's about nursin' the wounded and dyin' ... myneself will be weepin' most bittilee." She took her cap off, hid her face in it and started sniffing. "Myneself be so a-sad for the – uf-uf – sicklee soldiers."

Lofty, who was never very far away, re-appeared. He closed the medicine box, knelt down and took her hand. "Come, Littley. Larfter be the besterly medicine! Jowge! Be makin' us larf!"

George scratched his head. He couldn't think of a single joke – not a clean one, anyway. What could he do to cheer them up?

"I know – let's have a party!" he said. "Dad's at Bill's. Mum's out. Grandma's deaf. We can make as much noise as we like!"

Eave clapped her hands excitedly. "A party?

Think what fun, Pappy! But, alack... Us has no party cake."

She hung her head, but George saw her winking at Lofty.

"'Tis true, Littley!" insisted Lofty. "Us cannot be a-partyin' if us has no party cake."

They stood there with their arms folded, smiling hopefully at George.

"All right," he grinned. "You've made your point. I'll go and fetch you one."

CHAPTER FOUR

LAUGHTER
AND LADDERS

George let himself out of the attic and went
back down to the kitchen. He happened to
know there was a family-sized jam-and-cream
sponge in a box in the cupboard. If his mother
asked where it had gone, he'd say Grandma
had eaten it. It would be almost true, because
he was planning to give her a slice after the
party to cheer her up.

Should he take a box of icing sugar as well?
He had to really. A party cake ought to be
iced and decorated, otherwise it was just a
... cake. He took the tube of silver balls, the
pot of glacé cherries and the little bottle of

food colouring and stuffed everything into a carrier bag then made his way up the three flights of stairs back to his bedroom.

He could hear music coming from behind the green door. It was very faint, but it was definitely music; old-fashioned, crackly music. What was it coming from? There was no electricity in the loft and it wasn't from the piano.

He knocked and the music stopped. Eave opened the door a tiny crack, then ushered him in. She was dressed in a pink feather boa, a swimming cap covered in rubber flowers and a party dress made out of a silk petticoat covered in ruffles.

"Pappy, us guest be here!" she called excitedly, whirling her plaits.

"Is himself bringin' party cake, Littley?"

George showed her the sponge and her gooseberry-green eyes grew rounder and rounder.

"Yay! Jowge has be-fetched us a most normous cake ... with jam and cream!" She let him in, scolding him slightly for not dressing up in his party best.

"I didn't have time. I got you these, though," he said, passing the decorations to Eave.

Eave tipped the silver balls into her hand and poked them with a curious finger. "Whyfor be these marbils so smincey, Jowge?"

"They're not marbles. They're to decorate the cake with. And see this? It's icing sugar. Mix it with water, add a drop of this food colouring and you get blue icing," he told her. "Oh, and the sticky red things in the pot are glacé cherries."

"Cheeries, icin' and ebidle marbils!" gasped Eave. "Ooooh, such riches!" She hurried off with the cake and the bag of decorating stuff to the part of the attic that the Goffins had turned into a kitchen.

Lofty was standing on a chair, hanging strings of cloth bunting around the place. The flags were a bit dusty and they smelt of mildew but it all looked very festive.

"Darst say your great-great-granplods be usin' these same trimmin's when themselves be celebratin' Armistice Day, Jowge."

George looked at him blankly; history really wasn't his best subject. He had sat next to Warren in history and they spent the whole time playing battleships in their exercise books or flicking bits of inky paper at the girls. He wished he'd paid more attention now; he didn't want Lofty to think he was ignorant.

"Armistice Day be the end of Worldly War One, as no doubt yourself be knowin'," continued Lofty. "That be the war to end all wars, peepil did say. Oh-nee themselves be havin' another war shortly after ... whyfor Jowge?"

Fun and Games

"I don't know!" said George. "It wasn't me who started it!"

Lofty smiled at him fondly. "Nay. Yourself be peacefill Jowge. Fightin' and a-killin'? 'Tis not the Goffin way. Us be likin' it peacefill mostly."  He took off his pith helmet and replaced it with a Turkish fez, which perched on top of his wild, red hair like a robin in a gorse bush.

"Us be likin' dancin' and merrimakin' too, but us be livin' in dread of Them Below cotchin' us. Thus, 'tis rare for a Goffin to be lettin' his hair down..."

George noticed there were several hardened blobs of butter in Lofty's fringe, which made it stick up at an even madder angle than usual. It seemed rude to mention it, so he asked him about the music instead.

"Aha!" said Lofty. "Us has a windyfone. Come see, Jowge." He led George back into the parlour. There was a large object on the table, concealed under an old eiderdown.

"Myneself be hidin' it hastilee when yourself did knock, for fear it be somebiddy else," explained Lofty.

"But I used the knocking code we agreed on: *Pom ... tiddy pom ... pom pom.*"

George demonstrated on the table.

"Yourself did miss out a *pom*," insisted Lofty. "Us darst not be too carefree." He whisked away the eiderdown, revealing an antique wind-up gramophone with a beautifully polished wooden base and a brass horn in the shape of a flower. There was a record sitting on the turntable with '78' written on the label.

Fun and Games

"Itself be called the Charleston," said Lofty. "Darst say ye olde fambily Carruthers be a-dancin' to this same choon betwixt the wars."

George hadn't heard of the Charleston but he knew quite a bit about old records; his friend Jermaine collected them. His dad had built him a mixing desk to play them on and he used to "scratch" old records together with new ones to create a different sound, like a DJ.

Grandma had a record player in her room. It was over forty years old but at least it was electric. George was dying to see how the wind-up gramophone worked. "Play it again, Lofty!" he cried.

Lofty turned the handle. After the gramophone needle had bounced over a couple of scratches in the record grooves, it began to play the crackled, jazzy tune that George had heard through the green door earlier. As soon as she heard it, Eave came out of the kitchen and danced into the parlour, kicking her legs in the air. She grabbed George's hands and swung him around. "Come, Jowge. Myneself be learnin' you the Charleston, yay?"

77

Fun and Games

George wasn't the world's
greatest mover. He'd
refused to dance
at the school disco
because he felt so
embarrassed, but it
was impossible to
feel shy in front
of Lofty and
Eave. After a few
false moves, he found that he could
easily master the steps and he began
to regret all the parties he'd been
to where he just sat
like a lemon.

"Yourself
be a-groovin!"
encouraged Eave.
"Razzamatazz,
Jowgey!"

"Razzamatazz,
Eave!"

George was really getting into it when the music stopped.

"Itself be needin' a-windin'," said Lofty. "'Tis no bother."

It bothered George though. It was a nuisance having to keep winding the handle and he was glad technology had moved on. He had grown up with CDs and often downloaded tunes to listen to on his MP3 player. He would lend it to Lofty and Eave but he wasn't entirely sure they'd be able to work it.

"It doesn't have to be like this," he told Lofty. "I'll give you my old radio. All you have to do is switch it on and it'll play music for hours and hours. Weeks. Months, even."

Lofty's eyes lit up. "A raidi-who? Myne own ears be hardly believin' it ... months, even?"

"'Tis a windy-up, Pappy," laughed Eave.

"No, that's the whole point. You don't have to wind it up," said George. "It'll play until the batteries run out. You'll be able to listen to the news too."

"Pappy! George be fetchin' us new news!" she whooped.

They wanted him to fetch the radio straight away. To hear the latest news would be wonderful. Occasionally, Lofty would roof-fish for papers, but often all he caught was old news.

The Goffins had to rely on George to tell them what was going on in the world, but he didn't know the half of it. He'd been making a real effort lately to catch up but it was awfully hard to understand what the politicians were going on about, so he mostly stuck to the weather.

"Jowge, myneself be beggin' you to be-fetch the raidi-who now!" wheedled Eave.

"Let me see how you've decorated the cake first," he said.

Eave grabbed his hand and led him into the kitchen. It was George's favourite place in the attic.

Fun and Games

It was put together with
odd bits of furniture
and equipment that
had nothing to do
with kitchens and this
made it even more
interesting. There was
a French wardrobe for
a food cupboard. An
African shield was a fruit
bowl. An antique jewellery
box with quilted drawers
held eggs – pigeons' eggs laid
by Chimbley, whose nest was
in a pie dish up in the rafters.
The table top where Eave
did the food preparation was
originally his great-grandpa
Sid's old carpenter's
bench. On this sat
the party cake.

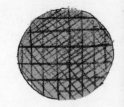

"Does yourself be likin' it, Jowge?" asked Eave, wringing her hands hopefully.

She'd added so much food colouring, the icing had turned almost black. She'd used the whole packet of silver balls, all the glacé cherries and stuck a funny ornament on top: a china dog pushing a puppy in a cart.

"Wow!" said George. "It's ... amazing!"

Fun and Games

Eave smiled her huge, bright smile. "Yay, myneself be icin' it most prettilee!" she said proudly. "Us be cuttin' it now, yay?"

George looked at the array of spectacular knifes hanging on the kitchen wall. They weren't chef's knives, they were weapons that Great-Great-Grandpa Montague had collected on his trips in Victorian times: flint axes from Australia; crop scythes from India; sacrificial daggers from Bali. Which of these would be best for slicing through a jam-and-cream sponge?

George chose a Japanese short sword with a jewel-encrusted handle. He was just about to cut the cake when something heavy banged twice against the window in the loft.

Eave screamed silently, ducked down
behind the carpenter's bench and pulled him
with her. George could feel her trembling. She
peered through her fingers in terror.

"Alack! Them Below be a-comin' up!"

Lofty had heard the banging too. He took
one look at the skylight and began to panic.

"Ladder! 'Tis a ladder! Trash and hide, trash
and hide!"

George's stomach lurched. His dad had
said he was going round to Bill's to watch
the football and fetch a ladder. It had never
crossed his mind he might use it to check
the roof.

Somehow, George had to stop him
climbing up.

CHAPTER FIVE

MARBLES AND MAYHEM

The top of the ladder banged against the sill of the skylight again. It was too late to hide. In her desperation, Eave had zipped her head inside George's sweatshirt and was clinging round his waist so tightly he could hardly breathe.

"Uf-uf – whatever – uf-uf – shall us do?" she sobbed.

George wasn't sure, but she was clearly expecting him to save her. Unzipping his top, he lifted up her chin. She was so frightened, her freckles had gone pale. "Eave, I promised to look after you so I will," he pledged.

Fun and Games

Suddenly George had an idea. It might not work, but he had to give it a try. "Quick, pass me the party cake. Lofty, give me your marbles. Now go and hide. Don't make a sound until I get back, OK?"

They tiptoed off, but then Eave turned round and gazed at him with mournful eyes. "Whatfor if yourself be never comin' back, Jowge?"

Lofty reached out and took her hand. "Hush, myne Littley. Jowge be a Carruthers! Carrutherses be lionbrave, yay? Himself be comin' back."

George answered in what he hoped was a confident and manly way. "Yep, you haven't seen the last of me. I'm a lionbrave Carruthers, I am."

Eave waved a tearful goodbye and melted into the darkness with her father. George hurried off. He was touched by Lofty and Eave's enormous faith in him, but the pressure was awful. What if he couldn't stop his father in time? It didn't bear thinking about. He stuffed the marbles in his pocket, charged all the way downstairs with the cake and ran into the garden.

"Daaaaaad!" he called.

His father was halfway up the ladder. When he heard George shout, he lost his footing and, for a moment, it looked like he'd plummet onto the patio outside Grandma's room.

Fun and Games

Luckily he managed to grab hold of the drainpipe to steady himself. He glanced down angrily.

"Whaaat?"

"Dad, come down! I need to show you something."

His father sounded like he wanted to kill him. "Can't it wait?"

"Not really. I made you this," said George, cheerily. He held up the party cake. "It's to ... say sorry for ... well ... not coming to watch the game with you."

It wasn't a total lie. He hadn't made the cake – let alone for his dad – but he *was* genuinely sorry about the football match.

"Oh." His dad seemed lost for words. He came down the ladder shakily and stared at the cake in disbelief.

"Sorry the icing's a bit black," said George. "I slipped with the food colouring."

"It's not that."

His dad touched the china dog ornament. "It's Bernie and Pooh."

"Bernie and who?"

"Pooh. Bernie and Pooh – those are the names of the dogs. My mum put that ornament on my fifth birthday cake."

"Grandma Peggy, you mean?"

"Yep... I'll never forget that party," he said. "We played parlour games, we had jelly and ice cream and my dad – your Grandpa Gordon – put a record on. One of his rock and roll ones. We played musical bumps..." He snapped out of his little memory trip. "Sorry, son. Nothing worse than your old dad banging on about his childhood."

George shook his head. "No, go on. I think it's really interesting."

Fun and Games

His father looked at him suspiciously, as if
he were being sarcastic. "Really? You never
used to. In fact, you used to put your hands
over your ears."

"Yeah, well, I've changed since we moved to
Grandma's," said George.

Meeting Lofty and Eave had changed him
in all sorts of ways. George liked to think
he'd become a bit more responsible and
grown-up, what with having to provide for
them and protect them. Maybe his parents
hadn't noticed the improvement in him yet
– particularly after his outburst this morning
– but he was working on it.

"How is Grandma, by the way?" asked his
dad. "Did you go and sit with her?"

"Course I did," said George. "She's feeling
really fed up, you know? Her knees are really
hurting. We should go and sit with her, Dad.
Give her some cake. Chat to her and that."

His father looked up at the roof. "You go.
I'll be along later. I really ought to check for

missing slates before the winter."

George's heart sank. His dad was about to go back up the ladder again, so he pleaded with him.

"It's only August, Dad! What's more important, slates or Grandma? Anyway, you almost fell off just now. You should have a sit-down. You might be in shock."

His dad took his foot off the bottom rung. "All right then. I didn't get anything to eat at Bill's. I could have some of that sponge."

"I'll put it in the fancy basket," said George. "Won't be a sec."

He went off to the kitchen. Grandma insisted on having her food served in a certain basket with a fancy handle.

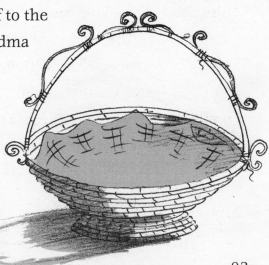

Fun and Games

She always put any leftovers outside on the bird table – for her little friends, the birds, she said. Maybe it was true, but George had an idea she was really leaving it out for Lofty and Eave.

George left the kitchen and found his father sitting next to Grandma's bed, but they weren't talking to each other. She was still in a foul mood and there was a bit of an atmosphere.

"What have you woken me up for?" she snorted. "I don't like cake with jam. It sticks to my dentures but does anyone listen? No, they don't when you're eighty."

"I made it for Dad," said George. "He was going to inspect the roof." George stressed the word roof, hoping that if Grandma knew about Lofty and Eave, she'd cotton on to what he was trying to tell her. But Grandma ignored his gaze completely.

George tried again. "Dad was halfway up the ladder ... which he'd leant against the attic window."

Grandma blinked slowly, then she pulled at his dad's elbow. "Here, Phillip! What do you want to go up there for?"

His father explained about needing to check the slates.

Fun and Games

"No need!" insisted Grandma. "Nothing wrong with them. I paid for that roof to be re-tiled out of my own purse before I went into hospital ... where's that cake, boy? I can always scrape the jam off."

George could have sworn Grandma winked at him, but she might have had something in her eye. He showed her the party cake. When she saw it, she sat up and clapped her hands.

"Oh, will you look at that? It's Bernie and Pooh! Where'd you find them, boy?"

"Kitchen cupboard," lied George. Grandma gave him a sideways look. "I'm sure I asked my Gordon to put them in the loft. Never mind, he didn't always do as he was told. He was a bit like you, boy, in that respect."

Out of the corner of his eye, George could see Bill's ladder rising slowly into the air. Lofty must be standing out in the roof garden pulling it up! What if his dad saw what he'd just seen? He had to distract him. George thrust a cake knife into his dad's hand. "You cut it!" he said, over-enthusiastically.

Now Grandma had seen the ladder too, George was sure. Lofty must be struggling with it. The legs kept going up a few inches, then dropping down again. George prayed that Grandma wouldn't say anything to give the game away.

"Close your eyes and make a wish, Phillip!" she barked.

George's father closed his eyes obediently. If he was only pretending to make a wish, George certainly wasn't.

Fun and Games

He was wishing with all his heart that Lofty would hurry up and shift the ladder before his dad opened his eyes again. Unfortunately, the ladder wasn't moving, so George had to think of a new way to keep his father's attention away from the window.

"Dad, see Bernie and Pooh? Their names are written under their bums ... see?" George picked the ornament off the cake and showed his father the underside. His dad smiled wistfully, picked the crumbs off and handed it to Grandma.

"You put them on my fifth birthday cake, remember, Mum?"

Grandma tapped the side of her head and pulled a face. "Yes, I'm not daft. I haven't lost my marbles yet, Phillip."

Marbles! George felt in his pockets. If he challenged his father to a game now, it would keep him occupied long enough for Lofty to pull the ladder right up to the attic without it being seen.

"Want to play, Dad?"

"Marbles? Hey, I haven't played that in years. I was the school champion. I beat Ben Raeside and won his Kingy ... you know what a Kingy is?"

George shook his head.

"A Kingy is the biggest marble you can get," said his dad. "The one I won off Ben was so heavy it wore a hole in my trouser pocket."

"I had to mend it," added Grandma. She pulled George's hand towards her to examine his marbles. "Show me... They don't make 'em like that any more, boy. Those look like the stoppers from the old stone bottles my father used to buy his lemonade in. Proper lemonade it was then, made from lemons. Not like nowadays."

She asked George where he'd got the marbles from.

"London," said George.

"London? Is that a fact?" asked Grandma. "Well, I never." Her eyes flicked quickly to the ladder, which had risen another few inches but was still clearly visible through the French windows.

"On your knees, Phillip!" she commanded. "Play on the carpet. Give the lad a game! You're not scared of losing, are you?"

His father needed no encouragement. George shared the marbles out and, making sure his father had his back to the window, they began to play. The marbles kept rolling under the bed and George's dad hit his head on the TV. Another time, during a very tricky drop shot, one of George's marbles plopped into Grandma's cold cup of cocoa that she'd left on the floor, but it was all very sporting; nobody got cross, nobody argued.

Grandma was keeping score, which was quite interesting because she seemed to be prolonging the game deliberately. Luckily, George's dad didn't notice or care. He was enjoying himself so much, he looked most disappointed when Grandma finally called time. George glimpsed out of the window. The ladder had gone. He took Grandma's hand and shook it.

"Well played, Grandma!" George said.

Grandma rolled her eyes. "You're meant to shake your opponent's hand, not mine, boy."

George's father held his hand out. "Well played, George ... re-match? Best of three?"

George really wanted to get back to the attic to reassure Lofty and Eave that the danger had passed but his father seemed to have no intention of ending the game. Just as George reluctantly agreed to yet another round, Grandma pointed to the window and shrieked, "Phillip, I just saw someone take your ladder! Quick, go after them!"

George's dad sprang to his feet, looked out of the window and swore.

"Bill will kill me!" he said. "He needs that ladder. Which way did they go?"

"Round the back and down the street!" shouted Grandma. "Go on! You might be able to head them off in the alley. We'll save you a bit of cake."

As his father skidded off, George was finding it very hard not to laugh. He put Lofty's marbles back in his pocket. To his surprise, Grandma was chuckling too.

"Who took the ladder, Grandma?" George asked. "What did they look like?"

She rubbed her knees and groaned. "Eh? How should I know, boy? Haven't got my specs on. You can't leave anything lying about these days."

Fun and Games

Grandma told him to cut a big slice of cake for his dad and mum.

"I'll give Mum two slices," said George. "She deserves it. She saves people's lives, you know."

George really wanted to tell her how proud he was of his mum and Agnes and Great-Great-Grandma Maud, the lionbrave suffragette, but he couldn't. Grandma would want to know how he knew and he could hardly say that Lofty and Eave had told him. So he asked her a question instead.

"Did you have a job in the olden days, Grandma?"

She smiled and said it had been a full-time job being a housewife and a mother. "But I did drive an ambulance during the war."

"First World War?" asked George innocently.

She clipped him playfully round the head. "Cheek! I'm not that flipping old. *Second* World War. I drove bomb victims to hospital.

It was a terrible business, but I wanted to do my bit."

George said she deserved an extra slice of cake too in that case, but she refused it.

"I shan't have any. Not keen on jam," she said. "Do me a favour, boy. Before you go, put my slice on the bird table, will you?"

"In the fancy basket with the handle ... or just loose?" asked George, guessing what the answer would be.

"Basket!" she said.

CHAPTER SIX

RAPPING AND ROCKING

George took what was left of the party cake back up to the attic, along with his old portable radio. It was only pocket-sized and not even digital. It had been a free gift from his mum's dress catalogue, but to Lofty and Eave it was priceless.

George handed it to Lofty who turned it over and over in his hands in amazement. Eave watched as he nervously extended the little aerial.

"Jowge, whyfor does the raidi-who be havin' a tail like the metal hound?" she asked.

"It helps to pick up the radio waves," he said.

Fun and Games

"Itself be wavin?" frowned Eave. "Nay!"

Eave didn't begin to understand the science of sound and as George had no idea how to explain it, he switched the radio on and showed her how to tune it in instead. It crackled between stations before settling on one that was playing a Bollywood song.

"Hark, Littley!" laughed Lofty. "This raidi-who be singin, in a most strange langwidge."

"I think it's something Indian," said George.

Eave's eyes widened. "'Tis Indian, Pappy! Jowge, us be knowin' muchly about India. Great-Great-Grandpappy Montague did travil there. Himself be savaged by a normous leopard."

"'Twas a tigger not a leopard," insisted Lofty. "Himself be fightin' a leopard in the Rockies."

"Nay, in the Rockies, 'twas a grizzlin' bear," argued Eave. "Great-Great-Grandpappy Montague did lose his small piggy! The leopard did swolly it whole."

"'Twas a tigger," grumbled Lofty.

Fun and Games

It seemed to George that his Great-Great-Grandfather had spent most of his youth being attacked by various savage beasts. According to what he'd read in the almanac, he'd battled with a polar bear, been half-suffocated by a python and here he was again having his foot mauled by a man-eating big cat of some description.

Eave fiddled with the tuning dial on the radio again. A man with a posh English voice was reading the local news. Eave screwed up her nose. "This talkin' be borin'. Myneself be wantin' happy choons."

She was about to twiddle the dial again

when Lofty held up his hand. "Hark! Himself on the raidi-who be speakin' of goin's-on in a church belfry! Darst say it be the same one Granny Cloister be livin' in with myne Ariel and myne oh-nee son Arch! 'Tis in this same county!"

Eave fell silent. They both pressed their ears to the radio and listened intently – it was an extended story about a local news event.

"What's he saying?" asked George. "Is it the belfry where your mum and brother live?"

"The raidi-who be sayin' that yesternights, two hooligins be arrested for tryin' to hook the bells from the belfry – ha! Themselves never did reckin on Goffins livin' above! Daresay myne Arch did sneak up and cotch 'em and fill them with dread!"

Fun and Games

"Myneself be bettin' Grandmuppy Cloister did blam themselves with her stick!" laughed Eave. "Herself be 103 winters old, Jowge!"

"104!" corrected Lofty. "Yesternights herself be havin' a birthday, remember?"

George managed to hear more of the news report. The youths claimed they were ramblers who'd got lost in the dark and on hearing strange music and laughter coming from the ruined church, had gone inside to investigate.

Lofty slapped his thigh and grinned.

"Myneself be thinkin' that noise be the sound of myne own fambily a-partyin'!"

"Yay!" said Eave. "That noise be myne muppy Ariel throwin' a fine birthday party for Grandmuppy Cloister." Her eyes shone brightly as she recalled the wonderful parties her mother had organized in the past.

"Herself always be bakin' a fine cake and makin' gifts, and us be havin' games and choons and dancin'. Grandmuppy be lovin' to dance, Jowge!"

George was surprised. "She's 104 years old and she can still dance?"

"Yay! Herself be doin' the Shmaltz." George had never heard of it.

113

"'Tis like a waltz, oh-nee it be sweeter and slower," explained Lofty. "Hush, or us will miss what himself on the raidi-who be sayin' next..."

"The music appeared to be coming from the belfry," confirmed the newsreader. "But upon entering, the alleged thieves claim they were chased back down the spiral staircase by a small but terrifying apparition making a hideous hooting noise."

Lofty clutched his sides and spluttered with laughter while Eave fell on her back, kicked her legs in the air and rolled around, giggling hysterically.

"What's so funny?" asked George.

"The ... hee ... hee! The ... ha ... the ... ho ... the ghoost be funny, Jowge!"

George still didn't get it.

"'Twas never a ghoost!" explained Lofty, drying his eyes. "That be myne oh-nee son Arch! Myneself be thinkin' Arch did besguise himself in an olde sheet and be makin' a spookfill rumpus by a-hootin' on his twigaloo. Thus himself be scarifyin' the dreaded villins yonder!"

115

Fun and Games

George was just about to ask what a twigaloo was when Eave stopped giggling. She sat up and and looked at him with a very solemn face.

"What's up?" asked George, "The police didn't see Arch, did they?"

"Nay ... but whatfor if themselves be comin' back..." She trailed off and her lip began to wobble.

"Come, Littley," said Lofty, drawing her to his side. "Don't be frettin'."

"But Pappy, myneself be so a-scared for myne fambily. Myneself be missin' them terrible. Yourself be most lucky, Jowge. Your fambily be safe!"

In the past, George had always thought his family were a bit of a pain. There were days when he wished they'd all go away and leave him alone, but the more Eave told him about them, the more he began to appreciate them.

He thought of the brilliant birthday parties his mum gave him when they lived in London.

She made him wonderful cakes and cooked special party food even though she must have been tired after working all day, saving lives. And even though his dad was always telling him to turn his music down, he'd bought him an MP3 player. And they let his mates stay for a sleepover, even though Warren once ate too much pizza and threw up from the top bunk all over Dino and Jermaine. His parents were very good to him really.

Fun and Games

George had taken it for granted that his parents would always be there for him and they'd all stay together. Eave and Lofty had been away from the rest of their family for two whole years.

No wonder Eave worried about them. George realized he'd miss his own family dreadfully if they had to live apart. If only there was something he could do to reassure Eave.

"If your family are ever in any danger ... well ... I'll rescue them!" said George rashly. "That's what I'll do! You just tell me where they are and I'll get on my bike and I'll go and rescue them .... just as soon as I've mended the puncture on the front tyre."

"Thanklee, Jowge," said Lofty. "Here's hopin' it never be comin' to that, though. Myne fambily be safe as squills in yonder saplin' so long as themselves has Arch. Arch be foxsharp. Arch be bulltough. Arch be lionbrave!"

"Yay!" said Eave, cheering up slightly. "Arch be eaglestrong. Himself be myne hero!"

"Eave, you're so lucky to have Arch," sighed George. He felt jealous. Apart from wanting to be a hero, he'd always wanted an older brother.

Eave looked at George thoughtfully, then slapped herself on the wrist as if to punish herself for not counting her blessings.

"Oh, Jowge, myneself be most lucky! Myneself has Arch and yourself. You be myne step-in brother, yay?"

And she was his step-in sister; they'd agreed that shortly after they first met, when they'd both confessed to being lonely. George stopped feeling jealous and decided that if he couldn't have a big brother himself, he could at least behave like a big brother to Eave. OK, she wasn't his real sister but she was a real Goffin; not every boy could claim that he'd been adopted by Goffins.

"Cake!" he said, suddenly. "This is meant to be a party. Let's have the cake now shall we? I'm sorry there isn't much left, but dad ate loads and I cut an extra slice for Mum – to try and make up for me calling her a bad mother this morning."

Eave looked at him with a mixture of fondess and relief.

"Myne step-in brother be doin' a Kindness – hurrah!" said Eave. "Did ... um ... Grandmuppy Peg be likin' us party cake?"

George looked at her sideways. Did she want to know if Grandma Peggy had put the cake out for the birds so that Lofty could roof fish for it later?

"She loved it," said George. "She ate every last crumb."

Eave's face fell and George grinned to himself.

"I'm lying, Eave. Grandma doesn't like jam. She made me put her slice on the bird table."

"Did yourself be puttin' it in the fancy basket be-chance?" asked Lofty.

George nodded. The Goffins tried not to look too pleased but now that they knew there'd be more party cake later, they couldn't quite hide their smiles.

They sat and ate the cake and listened to the radio. George had tuned it to a station that played rap music. It was his favourite ... or he always said it was, because he wanted to be like his friend Jermaine.

Fun and Games

Jermaine loved gangsta rap and everyone liked Jermaine, so George figured that if he pretended to like rap, they'd like him too. What he'd failed to realize was that the music had nothing to do with it; Jermaine was funny and clever and really good at sport.

They were listening to a song by a musician called Biggy Large. The lyrics were interesting and the beat was good and Lofty started tapping his feet, but suddenly Biggy Large said a swear word. Lofty dropped his cake and George leapt up and clapped his hands over Eave's ears.

"Whyfor be yourself mufflin' myne ears, Jowge?"

"It's ... er ... a bit rude..." he said.

While George had been quite happy to shock his parents with Mr Large's songs, he felt very protective of his step-in sister and didn't want her to hear bad language. He grabbed the radio and switched it to another station. It was playing rock and roll.

"That's better," he said. "It's a nice old song – not sure who's singing it though."

"Doesn't yourself be knowin' nothin'?" said Eave. "'Tis Elvis Parsley!"

"Himself be singin' about shoes, Jowge," explained Lofty. "Themselves be made from blue swedes – most smart, myneself darst say."

"Yay," added Eave. "Us can be doin' anything, but us darst not be treadin' on his blue swede shoes."

The song finished and the DJ came back on. "And that was Elvis Presley singing his great old hit, 'Blue Suede Shoes'!"

George looked at Lofty and Eave in amazement. "How come you know about Elvis Presley?"

"Us has mostly all his records," said Lofty. "Themselves be your grandpappy Gordon's."

Eave held up an old LP in a cardboard cover with a photo of a young Elvis Presley on the front, with his hair slicked back. In the corner of the cover was a sticky label. Someone had written their name on it in biro.

GORDON CARRUTHERS

George guessed that his Grandpa Gordon must have labelled his collection so that his records didn't get lost when he took them to parties. He wouldn't have been a grandfather in those days, of course. He'd have been a youngish man married to Peggy.

Grandpa Gordon had died over a year ago. George had never got to know him when he was alive. He regretted that now, but bit by bit he was learning about him from Lofty and Eave, and he was certain he would have liked him.

"Jowge? Yourself must be givin' 'Blue Swede Shoes' to Grandma Peggy," said Eave. "Herself be full of miseree, yay? Herself be missin' parties and dancin' with Grandpa Gordon."

"Her knees are really playing up," said George. "She's not like Granny Cloister. She can't dance any more, I'm afraid."

"That may be dependin' on the choon, Jowge," said Lofty, quietly.

Just then, the radio crackled, then whistled, then it went silent. Eave shook it in dismay.

"Alack! Itself be deaded, Jowge!" she cried. "Whatever shall us do?"

CHAPTER SEVEN

TUNES AND TWIGALOO

Happily, the radio wasn't dead. The batteries had run out, that was all. George slid open the plastic compartment in the back and tipped them into his hand. Lofty took one, shook it next to his ear then spoke sharply to it.

"Speak to myneself! Whyfor be yourself not singin'?"

George tried to explain. "It's a battery, Lofty. It's just a thing that you put into ... er ... electric things to make them work if they haven't got a plug on."

"Aha!" said Lofty. "The tub where myneself do bathe be havin' a plug!"

The Goffins

George sighed
inwardly. "No,
not that sort of
plug ... I mean
the sort you
stick in a socket."

Lofty looked
confused but then
he rolled up the legs
of his oversized

explorer's shorts and displayed a pair of
woolly socks held up with regimental garters.

"Sockets!" he cried. "These be the self-same
sockets your great-great-uncool Cecil did wear
when himself was a Royal Horse Guard."

George gave up. It wasn't that Lofty was
dim, it was just that electricity was a difficult
concept to grasp – especially if you had
managed without it all your life.

"I'll bring you some new batteries
tomorrow," George said. "Then the radio
will play music again."

But tomorrow wasn't soon enough for Eave. "Us has no music now without the raidi-who. Howfor can us be partyin' with no choons?"

"We could still play music on your windyphone," said George. "But we'll have to keep an ear out for Dad. He could be back anytime."

Eave pulled her best sulky face. She'd lost interest in the gramophone. After listening to the radio's exciting new music and programmes, it seemed old-fashioned to her now.

"Whyfor must myneself be windin' handils when us could be twiddlin' knobs?"

"Now, Littley!" scolded Lofty. "Betterly an old-fangled friend than a new fangled foe!"

But George was on Eave's side. "It's all right," he whispered. "My dad likes the old things best too. Same as Grandma. It's because they can't keep up with the technology."

"Myne ears be a-flappin'!" said Lofty. "Hark!

Myneself be welcomin' the new, Jowge, but 'tis folly to be castin' away old treasures too hastily."

He made a slow, sweeping gesture with his hand, as if to point out all the wonderful relics that several generations of Carruthers hadn't had the heart to throw away.

"Myneself and Littley still be makin' goodly use of all this," he went on. "Some be the stuff us be dependin' on to stay alive: vessels, blankin's, clothin', tools, furniture, fuel ... all old, but all the better for it, Jowge."

Even George saw
that Lofty was right.
The furniture in the
attic was much more
solid than the modern
stuff his parents had.
The wood might be a
bit wormy in places but
it was real wood, dark
and shiny after years of
being lovingly polished.
He admired the tables
with their beautifully
carved lion feet
and decorations
inlaid with
mother-of-pearl.

As for the antique clothes, they might have been a bit moth-eaten, but they were hand-stitched, not made in a factory. They were made from natural material that felt good – so much nicer than the synthetic stuff most of his clothes were made from, George thought.

"Then there be treasures for makin' us joyfill," said Lofty. "Ye olde paintin's, the scribblin's, the games ... and ye olde music!"

He reached into his pocket and pulled
out a small wooden object, shaped like
a short, stout flute.

"Myneself be carvin' it from the tree
branch hangin' near yonder sky-like."

"What is it?" asked George.

"'Tis a twigaloo," said Lofty
proudly. "All sons of Goffins be
learnin' to play the twigaloo."
He blew down it softly. It made
a noise like an owl. "Myneself be
usin' it to lure most any wildfowl," he said.

Lofty changed the shape of his lips and this
time he made the twigaloo sound like a duck.

"'Tis usefill
for huntin'
when meat be
scarce," he said.
"'Tis also usefill
for warnin' that
somebiddy be comin'
from Down Below."

He blew sharply and produced a strange barking sound. It wasn't quite a dog's bark. George had heard the same sound the night he'd first moved into Grandma's house.

"'Tis a vixin yalp," explained Eave. A fox cry! So that night, when George first heard the sound, had it been a vixen in Grandma's garden? Or was it Lofty blowing his twigaloo? Lofty wasn't giving anything away.

"A Goffin without a twigaloo be

like a cockerill without a crow," he said. "'Tis
an olde, olde instrument. When myne ancient
rellies be livin' aloft in the trees of Inish Goff,
themselves did play sweet twigaloo choones
be-nightly."

He blew down the twigaloo again, running
his fingers quickly over the little holes, and
produced an eerie but beautiful tune. It
reminded George of a lullaby.

"Can I have a go?" he asked. "Will you teach
me, Lofty ... please?"

George had refused to learn the recorder
at school because he was scared his friends
would think he was a nerd. Well, he had new
friends now and he could join in with Lofty
and Eave by learning to play the twigaloo.

Lofty handed it to him. George ran his thumb over the barrel. It felt pleasingly smooth and was lovely to look at. It must have taken ages to whittle and to cut a reed the exact size to slip into the little slit in the mouthpiece.

George looked down the end of the twigaloo, then wiped the mouthpiece on his sleeve, puffed out his cheeks and blew hard. It sounded like someone blowing a really rude raspberry. Eave clapped her hand over her mouth.

"It be soundin' like Pappy after himself swollied Grandmuppy Peg's laxi-squits!"

Lofty put his finger to his lips and shushed her. "Nay larfin', Littley. Softlee, softlee, Jowge. Be puckerin' up like a muppy kissin' a bubby ... now huff like yourself be blowin' out a candil."

George concentrated on his breathing and, very gently, he produced his first note on the twigaloo. He held it so that it lingered and quavered. He didn't want it to stop and he held on and on until he ran out of breath and almost fainted.

"Oh, Jowge," sighed Eave. "Yourself be music to myne ears!"

"Himself be playin' like a true Goffin in no time!" announced Lofty. George didn't want to give the twigaloo back, but Eave demanded that Lofty played the Goffin National Anthem on it so that she could sing along.

"Us always be singin' the national anthem at parties," she declared. "Myneself be learnin' yourself the words, Jowge."

It was a rousing tune, all about the joys of living aloft, but just before the end, Lofty stopped. A look of panic flickered across his face and he quickly blew the vixen yelp.

"Is someone Down Below?" whispered George. Lofty nodded and tiptoed backwards into the darkest, most secret part of the attic.

"My dad must be back," sighed George. "I guess the party's over."

Eave smiled sadly and held out her arms. "'Twas myne besterly party ever. Thankly Jowge."

George wasn't in the habit of hugging girls, but Eave was different.

She was the little sister he'd always wanted.
He gave her a big squeeze and lifted her
off the floor.

She handed
him the Elvis
record. "For
Grandma
Peggy, yay?"
"Yay."
Yay? He
was even
starting to talk
like a Goffin.
"And Jowge?
Be givin' herself
a hotbottle for the
knacky knees. 'Tis a
goodly Goffin cure."
"I will."

Lofty reappeared and pressed something into his hand. "For myne step-in son," he said shyly.

It was the twigaloo. George felt his eyes welling up. "Are you sure, Lofty?" he asked. "It must have taken forever to make."

"'Tis myne partin' party gift," he said. "Mynself be swappin' it for the Kindness of raidi-who butteries. Yourself be bringin' them soon, yay?"

"Very soon," said George. "Tomorrow."

He waved goodbye and closed the attic door behind him, feeling all warm and glowy.

CHAPTER EIGHT

KICK-ABOUTS AND KINDNESS

George went downstairs to see Grandma
Peggy. She was still lying on the bed in her
nightie and she was still in a bad mood.

"What's up, Grandma?" asked George
brightly.

"I'm fed up!" she scowled. "It's no fun being
old, boy. I can't do anything I used to do. It
feels like the whole world's having a party and
I'm not invited."

George swallowed hard. Did she know
about the party, he wondered? Had she heard
them dancing and playing? He wished he
could have invited her, but how could he?

He'd never break his promise to Lofty and Eave about keeping them secret. And anyway, Grandma could never have managed the stairs to the attic and joined in.

"We should get Dad to put one of those stairlifts in," he said. "Would you like that?"

"Why would I?" she replied. "It not like there's anything going on upstairs, is there?"

She held him in her gaze, but he didn't crack. He waved the Elvis record at her instead.

"Got you this, Grandma. Shall I put it on your windyphone or whatever it's called?"

"It's a record player," she tutted.

But when she saw who was on the cover of the LP her expression softened.

"Is that Elvis? Oh, I do love him! So did your Grandpa Gordon. Where'd you find it, boy?"

"Behind my ... wardrobe," lied George. "Shall I play it for you?"

Grandma Peggy lay back on her pillows and pretended not to care. "You can do," she said. "Not that I can dance to it any more. Not with my knees."

George lifted the dusty lid off the record player, dropped the record onto the deck and put the needle in the groove.

"Don't scratch it, boy!" said Grandma. "'Blue Suede Shoes'? That was Gordon's favourite."

"I know," said George carelessly.

Grandma narrowed her eyes suspiciously. "How do you know? An educated guess, was it?"

It was Eave who'd told him! How could he wriggle out of what he'd just said without giving Lofty and Eave away?

145

The Goffins

"Grandma, what I meant was ... I know it's Blue Suede Shoes. Um ... I've got to go now."

"Why have you?"

Why had he? He couldn't think. "Well, I have to go because I have to ... put the kettle on to make Mum a cup of tea! Yes, then it will be ready for when she gets in from work ... saving lives."

He hurried off to the kitchen before she could question him any further. He hadn't been planning to make his mother a cup of tea, of course, but now he was in the kitchen he realized he could fill a hot-water bottle to sooth Grandma's knees – as a Kindness. Eave would be pleased with him. The kettle was just coming to the boil when his dad walked in.

"They got away with it, the beggars!" he said. "They escaped with Bill's ladder. I've been down to the Police Station but they don't want to know, so then I had to go to the hardware shop to buy a new one. Then I had to cart it round to Bill's, and then..."

His dad was going into a long moan-fest, so George offered to make him some tea. He felt bad about the ladder – especially as he knew exactly where it was and who had taken it.

George filled Grandma's hot-water bottle and made tea for his dad. He could make his mum a cup later. He might even spoil her and use the teapot and proper tea leaves instead of bags. Right now, his dad was his priority.

The Goffins

George thought he might like it if they drank tea together and had a conversation for once.

"How was the match, Dad?" he asked.

"Ah, it was really good. It was three all with five minutes to go, but then the ref—"

Suddenly, he stopped and looked at George with his head on one side. "Why are you asking? Thought you weren't interested."

"I am," said George. "I love football. I was just in a bad mood today."

"I loved playing when I was your age," said his dad. "They used to call me Bangbang Carruthers."

"Why?"

"Because I never stopped shooting. I scored more goals in one season than any player they'd ever had."

George
preferred
being in goal.
He was a pretty
good goalie – even
Jermaine said so
– but he was a bit out of
practice, what with having
no one to shoot at him.

"So ... you reckon you could
get one past me then, Dad?"

"Yep. They didn't call me
Bangbang Carruthers for nothing.
Tell you what, George, why don't
we have a kick-about in the garden
after Mum gets home?"

George was about to remind him that it
would be difficult without any football boots,
but then he realized it didn't matter. What
mattered was that for the first time in ages,
his dad had actually offered to play football
with him.

"Great!" he said. "Brilliant! I'll just wear my old trainers... What'll we do for a goal, Dad?"

"Your sweatshirt, my jumper. We'll pretend they're the posts, George. Like we did in the olden days. See you later, mate."

Mate? His dad had actually called him mate! George was in a brilliant mood now. He tucked the hot-water bottle under his arm and almost skipped back to Grandma Peggy's room. The door was shut so he pushed it open with his foot.

"Grandma!" he gasped.

She was standing in the middle of the room in her nightie. And she was dancing to 'Blue Suede Shoes'. As soon as she saw George, she stopped.

"What are you gawping at, boy?" she said. "Don't you ever knock? I'm doing my physiotherapy. My leg exercises. Doctor Murray said I had to." But she hadn't been doing leg exercises. She'd been dancing wildly to Elvis and her face was shining.

"That's enough of that, boy," she said. "Switch the record player off, will you?"

She limped back to
bed and George passed her
the hot-water bottle. "What do I want
that for? It's baking hot," she grumbled.

"For your sore knees?"

She looked pleasantly surprised. "Oh? Very
kind, I'm sure. Very thoughtful. So, what have
you been doing all afternoon?"

"Just playing."

"Made new friends have you?"
she sniffed. "Thought so. What've
you been playing?"

He wanted to tell her about
Spillikins, about the party and
the twigaloo. He wanted to tell
her everything, but of course he
couldn't.

"We played I-Spy," he said.

Grandma fiddled with the cuffs
on her nightie. "I-Spy? I thought you
only liked those horrible modern
games – the electriconic ones."

"Yeah, I know, but new things aren't
always best, are they?" He recited Lofty's
phrase, "Betterly an old fangled friend than
a new fangled foe, eh, Grandma?"

She refused to respond, but then she looked
him boldly in the eye and said, "I quite like
I-Spy."

George sat down next to her on the bed.
"Go on then, Grandma. I'll give you a game."

The Goffins

She rolled her thumbs and pretended to give it some thought. "All right then. Just as long as you don't cheat," she said. "Pass me my glasses, boy!"

They began to play, but even though Grandma was wearing her glasses, she never noticed a fishing line dangling over the bird table. She never even noticed the basket full of cake being hooked by the handle and reeled up, up into the sky.

Or did she?

Don't miss
Lofty and Eave
in book 1

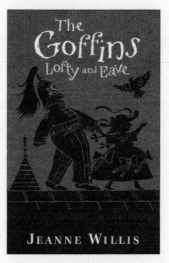

The whole summer at grumpy Grandma's house? Boring! But when George explores Grandma's attic he finds an exciting secret hidden among the moth-eaten clothes, family heirlooms and faded photographs...

He finds the Goffins!

Is there a Goffin in *your* attic?